An I CAN READ Book

THE
ELEPHANT
WHO COULDN'T
FORGET

by Faith McNulty
Pictures by Marc Simont

HARPER & ROW, PUBLISHERS

To my sisters, of course…

The Elephant Who Couldn't Forget
Text copyright © 1980 by Faith McNulty
Illustrations copyright © 1980 by Marc Simont
Printed in
the United States of America. For information address
Harper & Row, Publishers, Inc., 10 East 53rd Street,
New York, N.Y. 10022. Published simultaneously in
Canada by Fitzhenry & Whiteside Limited, Toronto.
First Edition

Library of Congress Cataloging in Publication Data
McNulty, Faith.
    The elephant who couldn't forget.

    (An I can read book)
    SUMMARY: Young elephant learns that he must remember
what to forget.
    [1. Elephants—Fiction.   2. Memory—Fiction]
I. Simont, Marc.   II. Title.
PZ7.M24El   [E]   79-2741
ISBN 0-06-024145-4
ISBN 0-06-024146-2 lib. bdg.

THE
ELEPHANT
WHO COULDN'T
FORGET

All elephants have good memories.

A young elephant named Congo

had a super memory.

As a baby, he remembered more
than other baby elephants.
At four he could remember
more than his brother, Zambesi,

6

who was six,

and almost as much

as his sister, Victoria,

who was eight.

His mother, Nyasa,

loved all her children,

but she was especially proud of Congo.

She said to Grandmother Manyara,

who was leader of their family,

"I am so proud of Congo.

He never forgets anything."

Huge old Manyara was resting,

fanning herself with her ears.

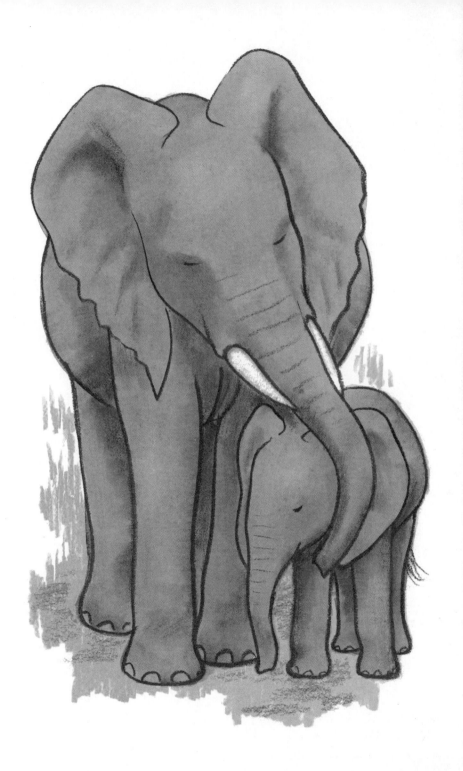

She spat out a wad of twizzle—

pieces of wood and bark

too tough to swallow—

and said, "That's very good.

If he remembers what is important."

Manyara lay down for her noon nap.

Congo, who was listening,

felt proud.

He resolved to try hard

to remember

that he must remember

what is important.

Noon in Africa is very hot.

The sun shines like a gold coin

in the sky.

Wise old Manyara had led her family

to a cool, leafy place to rest.

In an elephant family

the adult male elephants

live by themselves.

The grandmother is

the leader of the family.

Her daughters

and grandchildren follow.

She teaches them wisdom,

gathered during her long life.

Manyara was very old.

She had much to teach.

"Remember what's important,"
Congo said to himself,
as he lay down in the shade.
While the rest of the family snoozed,

14

Congo stayed awake,

thinking, and remembering

the things he had learned

about elephant life.

Lions.

He remembered lions.

One day his mother, Nyasa,

had smelled a lion nearby.

She flapped her ears

and stamped her huge feet,

raising clouds of dust.

With her trunk

she pulled little Congo

close to her side.

Manyara lifted her trunk

and gave a bugle call of warning.

She shook her huge head in rage

and charged into the bushes.

The lion slunk away.

After that, Congo remembered

the smell of a lion

and knew that a lion

is dangerous to a little elephant

who leaves his mother's side.

Food.

Congo thought about food.

He still sucked milk from his mother,

but he also ate fruit and flowers

and leaves and bark.

He remembered the day

his sister, Victoria, had shown him

how to use the tip of his trunk

like a finger...

to pick sweet flowers

without touching prickly thorns.

Manners.

Elephants have strict rules.

Baby elephants

are loved by their mothers,

aunts, grandmothers,

brothers and sisters,

and are allowed to have their own way.

But as they get older,

they are expected

to learn how to behave:

not to snatch food from an elder,

to wait in turn to drink water,

not to wake up a sleeping elephant,

not to play too rough

with any elephant

smaller than they are.

"I must remember all that,"

Congo said to himself.

The elephant family was waking up.

With a grunt and a rumble,

Manyara got to her feet.

She was twelve feet tall.

She weighed four tons.

Manyara wrapped her trunk
around a tall tree.
Its branches were too high
for a small elephant to reach.

26

Manyara pulled it up by the roots,

so that

Congo and Zambesi and Victoria

could eat the tender leaves.

Aunt Tanganyika

waked her baby, Limpopo,

with a loving pat.

Between her front legs,

big as tree trunks,

he found her milk and sucked.

Soon Victoria and Zambesi
began to play.
They wrestled and shoved,
pushed and chased,
rolled and tugged.
Congo joined the game.
They played like
huge, clumsy puppies.
Victoria and Zambesi
were careful not to hurt Congo,
because he was the smallest
of the three.

Elephants love water.

Manyara led the family

toward the lake for a bath

and a roll in the mud.

They moved slowly
on feet like big round cushions.
They ate while they moved,
snatching leaves along the path.
Their stomachs made a loud rumbling,
a friendly sound

that happy elephants often make.

At the lake

the elephants waded in

up to their knees.

The big elephants

sucked up gallons of water—

as much as a bathtub would hold.

They sprayed it over themselves

in cool, muddy showers.

Congo and Victoria and Zambesi

began to spray each other.

They splashed and pushed

and rolled in the shallow water,

having a wonderful time.

Then something went wrong.

Zambesi forgot the rules.

He pushed Congo down.

He squirted mud in his eye.

Congo screeched.

Zambesi pushed him underwater.

Congo's trunk stuck up like a snorkel

while he struggled to get free.

Nyasa and Victoria hurried to help.

They lifted poor Congo to his feet.

Congo coughed and snorted

while Nyasa rubbed his back.

"Zambesi is a bad brother

and a bad elephant,"

Congo screamed.

"And I'll never, never forget!"

All the rest of the day

Congo thought about bad Zambesi.

After their bath,

the family climbed the hillside

for supper.

In the sweet-smelling forest

figs were ripe on the trees.

With each bite of fruit

Congo thought,

"Bad Zambesi...I'll never forget."

Victoria and Zambesi

and little Limpopo began to play,

tugging and trumpeting and squealing

with fun.

Congo watched, muttering,

"Bad Zambesi...I'll never forget."

That night as he went to sleep,

tucked against

Nyasa's great, gray flank,

he murmured to himself,

"Never...never forget..."

When Congo woke in the morning,

he remembered Zambesi.

His breakfast of figs

didn't taste very sweet.

He didn't eat many.

Zambesi and Limpopo

began a new game.

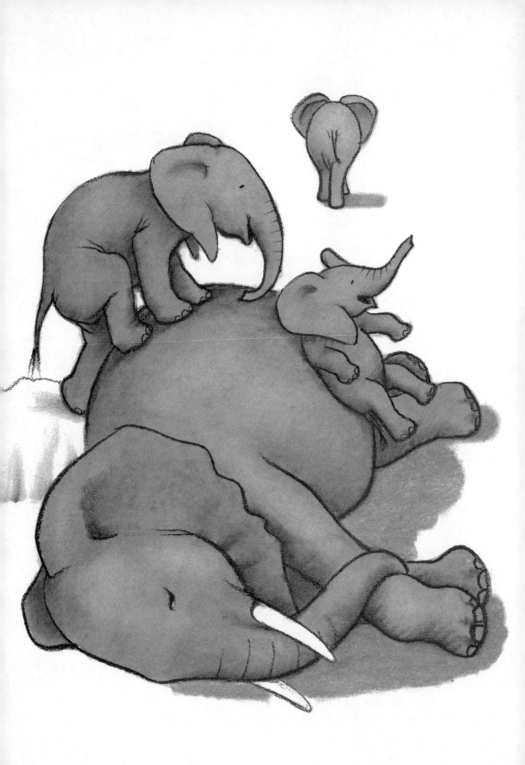

They climbed on Aunt Tanganyika,

who lay resting,

and slid down her steep, gray side.

Congo wanted to join in.

Then he thought,

"Never forget,"

and walked away.

All that day,

at lunchtime, nap time,

at swimming time and playtime,

and suppertime and bedtime,

Congo remembered.

Sometimes

he felt like forgetting,

but then he would remember

that he was Congo,

the elephant with the super memory,

and he would say to himself,

"Congo never, never forgets."

Days passed.

Sometimes

Zambesi invited Congo to play.

Congo would say,

"I have a super memory....

I never forget..."

and walk away.

Zambesi and Victoria and Limpopo

played together,

but they missed Congo.

Congo was growing thin.

His face sagged in sad wrinkles

as he muttered to himself,

"I have a super memory.

I never, never forget."

Grandmother Manyara

had been watching.

She called the family together.

They stood in a circle

while Manyara spoke.

"The family is not happy," she said.

"Zambesi and Victoria and Limpopo are lonely.

Congo doesn't eat. He doesn't play.

Perhaps Congo is sick."

"I'm not sick," Congo said.

"I have a super memory.

I can't forget what Zambesi did."

"I see," said Manyara.

She flapped her ears while she thought.

"I am old," she said.

"I remember more than any of you.

But there are things

even I have forgotten."

"What things, Grandmother?"

asked Congo.

"Things not worth remembering,"

said Manyara.

She pointed her trunk at Congo.

"You have a very good memory

for a little elephant, Congo,

but you have forgotten

the first lesson."

"What is that?" asked Congo.

"You have forgotten to remember

what is important," Manyara said.

"Sometimes, in order to remember

something important

you have to forget

something that isn't important."

Manyara gently pushed Congo

toward Zambesi.

"It is important to remember,"

she said, "that you and Zambesi

are brothers."

Zambesi's trunk reached out to Congo,

and Congo's reached out

and touched Zambesi.

Manyara lifted her head high

and gave a trumpet call.

It was a signal for the family
to follow her to the lake
to bathe and play.

Walking beside Zambesi,

Congo felt very happy.

"I have a super memory,"

he said to himself.

"And I will always remember

what to forget."